CB137310

Scan the QR code
to read and listen to the
glossary words for FREE!

glossary - Meanings of words.

Dados Internacionais de Catalogação na Publicação (CIP) de acordo com ISBD

B347w Baum, L. Frank
The Wonderful Wizard of Oz - Easier Classics Reading / L. Frank Baum. – Jandira : W. Books, 2025.
208 p. ; 12,8cm x 19,8cm. – (Easier Classics Reading Library Children's Collection)

ISBN: 978-65-5294-258-6

1. Literatura infantojuvenil. 2. Literatura Infantil. 3. Clássicos. 4. Aventura. 5. Imaginação. 6. Fantasia. I. Título. II. Série.

2025-610

CDD 028.5
CDU 82-93

Elaborado por Vagner Rodolfo da Silva - CRB-8/9410
Índice para catálogo sistemático:
1. Literatura infantojuvenil 028.5
2. Literatura infantojuvenil 82-93

Easier Classics
The Wonderful Wizard of Oz

Adapted Text © Every Cherry Publishing Limited, 2024
Inside Illustrations © Sweet Cherry Publishing Limited, 2024
Cover Illustrations © Sweet Cherry Publishing Limited, 2024

Original story by L. Frank Baum.
Text based on the adaptation by Gemma Barder.
Illustrations by Archina Laezza.

© 2025 edition:
Ciranda Cultural Editora e Distribuidora Ltda.

1st edition in 2025
www.cirandacultural.com.br
No part of this publication may be reproduced, stored in a retrieval system, or transmitted in any form or by any means, electronic, mechanical, photocopying, recording, or otherwise, without written permission of the publisher.
This book is a work of fiction. Names, characters, places, and incidents are either the product of the author's imagination or are used fictitiously, and any resemblance to actual persons, living or dead, business establishments, events, or locales is entirely coincidental.

THE WONDERFUL Wizard of Oz

L. Frank Baum

W. Books

Meet the Characters

Dorothy

Toto

Scarecrow

Lion

Tin Man

Aunt Em

Uncle Henry

The Wicked Witch of the West

The Good Witch of the North

Glinda

The Wizard of Oz

Chapter 1

Dorothy made her way to collect the morning's eggs. Following closely behind, was her little dog, Toto.

She often helped out on the farm, where she lived with her Aunt Em and Uncle Henry.

Their small wooden farmhouse was in the middle of the grey **Kansas prairies**.

Kansas - *A state in the middle the United States of America (USA).*

prairies - *A large, open area covered in grass.*

'Oh Toto,' sighed Dorothy. 'I wish that something exciting would happen!'

But when she looked around the prairie, she could see nothing but grass.

As Dorothy passed Uncle Henry, she saw that he was looking **nervously** at the sky.

nervously - *The way someone does something when they feel scared or worried.*

'Good morning, Uncle Henry!' said Dorothy.

'A storm is coming,' said Uncle Henry, anxiously. The clouds were looking greyer than usual.

'You'd better get inside,' he said, as he ran to check that the animals were safe.

Dorothy could see the grass blowing wildly as the storm got closer.

Dorothy went inside the farmhouse.

'Your uncle thinks we should head for the **storm shelter** soon,' said Aunt Em.

Suddenly, Uncle Henry ran through the front door and shouted, 'Cyclone!'

A cyclone was a huge tunnel of wind that twisted up to the sky. It damaged everything it touched. The only thing to do was hide and wait for it to pass.

storm shelter - An underground room used to protect people from bad storms.

Suddenly - Quickly and not expected to happen.

Uncle Henry and Aunt Em ran to hide in the storm shelter.

'Dorothy, quick!' shouted Uncle Henry, as the door blew shut behind him.

'Where's Toto?' cried Dorothy. The little dog was scared of the noise and had gone to hide in the farmhouse.

'I have to find him!' shouted Dorothy as she ran after Toto.

As the wind blew faster and faster around the house, something strange happened.

The wind began to move the house.

At first, the house shook from side to side. Then suddenly, it flew up into the air with Dorothy and Toto stuck inside!

Chapter 2

Dorothy shut her eyes and held onto the kitchen table. She was scared of falling out of the house!

All at once, the house landed with a **thud**.

The wind **disappeared**.

Everything was quiet.

thud - The noise made when something heavy hits the ground.

disappeared - Went away.

Dorothy slowly opened her eyes. Toto ran from his hiding place and jumped into her arms. She stepped outside carrying him.

Outside, she saw a rainbow of colours. The cyclone had left the farmhouse in a beautiful place.

The grass was green, the trees were filled with colourful fruit and pretty flowers grew everywhere.

Dorothy was not in Kansas.

Everything looked different and exciting. Nearby, there was a little stream with a bridge across it.

She made her way towards lots of colourful, tiny houses.

'Welcome to the Land of the **Munchkins**, witch!' said a lady with a kind face and white hair.

Munchkins - *The magical people who live in the Land of the Munchkins.*

Dorothy was surprised. She wasn't a witch!

Suddenly, Munchkins began to **appear** from behind the trees.

They were dressed in pointed hats and had bells on their shoes that jingled when they walked.

appear - When something is seen that wasn't there before.

'What is your name, my dear? Are you a good or bad witch?' asked the lady with the white hair.

'I'm not a witch,' said Dorothy. 'My name is Dorothy Gale. This is my dog, Toto.'

'It's lovely to meet you. I am the Good Witch of the North,' replied the friendly witch.

The Good Witch of the North smiled and said, 'The Munchkins told me that you killed the **Wicked** Witch of the East.'

'I haven't killed anybody!' Dorothy said, shocked.

'Your house did,' said the witch. Dorothy looked at her farmhouse. Sticking out from underneath it, were a pair of legs with sparkling silver shoes on their feet.

Wicked - Something evil or unkind.

'I didn't mean to kill anyone!' cried Dorothy.

The witch placed her arm around Dorothy and said, 'Don't worry. The Wicked Witch was evil and unkind to the Munchkins. Now they are free!'

Dorothy looked at the Munchkins.

They were very happy!

'What can we do to say thank you?' asked the witch.

'All I want is to go home,' said Dorothy sadly. 'Home to Kansas.'

'If that is your wish,' the witch said with a smile. 'Then you must go to the Emerald City to see the Great Wizard of Oz. They will help you.'

'Can't you use your magic to send me home?' Dorothy asked the witch.

'My magic isn't that strong,' said the witch.

The Good Witch pointed to Dorothy's feet. Dorothy's shoes had changed into the Wicked Witch of the East's sparkling, silver shoes.

'These shoes are **charmed**. They will **protect** you,' said the witch.

charmed - *Something that is protected by magic.*

protect - To look after.

The shoes fit Dorothy perfectly.
She felt safer wearing them.

'How do I get to the Emerald City?' asked Dorothy.

The Munchkins moved aside, **revealing** a path.

'Just follow the Yellow Brick Road,' said the witch smiling. 'It will lead you straight to the Emerald City and the Wizard.'

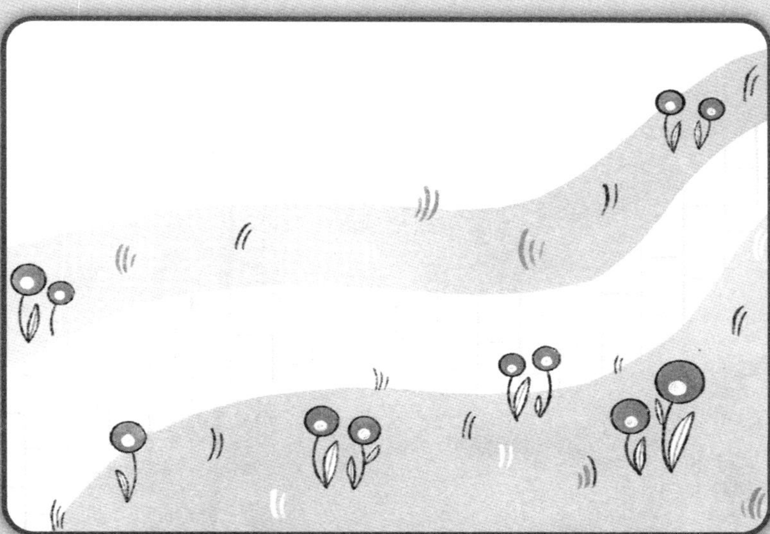

revealing - *Showing or saying something that wasn't known before.*

'There is just one thing you need to remember,' warned the witch.

'The Wicked Witch of the West will not be very happy that you dropped your house on her sister.

Watch out, she will want her sister's shoes. But, don't let her take them,' said the witch.

Dorothy took a step onto the bright yellow path in her sparkling, silver shoes. Toto followed, wagging his tail, ready for adventure.

Chapter 3

Dorothy and Toto walked down the Yellow Brick Road. It led to the countryside. They walked past huge fields of **corn**.

'I wonder how long it will take to get to the Emerald City?' she asked Toto. She felt scared and alone.

'The Emerald City?' asked a voice. 'It is a very long walk.'

corn - A plant which is grown in lots of fields in the USA. The plant grows into corn on the cob and sweetcorn.

Dorothy looked around. There was nothing but cornfields and a single **scarecrow** on a fencepost.

'Who said that?' Dorothy said.

'It was me!' said the scarecrow, surprising Dorothy.

A scarecrow had never spoken to her before!

scarecrow - Something that looks like a human but is filled with straw. It is used to scare birds away.

'How do you do?' said Dorothy.

'I'm not very well,' said Scarecrow. 'I'm stuck on this pole! Please could you help me?'

Scarecrow looked very friendly. He wore an old pair of dungarees with bits of straw sticking out of his body.

Dorothy stepped closer and pulled out the nail that held him to the pole.

'Phew! That does feel better,' said Scarecrow.

He **stumbled** as he tried to walk. Dorothy thought it was probably because he had straw for legs.

'I need to go now,' said Dorothy. 'I am on my way to the Emerald City to meet the Wizard.'

stumbled - When someone trips or falls when they walk.

'The Wizard of Oz?' asked Scarecrow. 'They say the Wizard is very powerful. Do you think I could come with you?'

Scarecrow **explained** that he had always wanted a brain because his head was filled with straw.

Dorothy was happy to let Scarecrow, her new friend, come with her.

explained - *To help someone understand something.*

Dorothy and Scarecrow walked along the Yellow Brick Road.

They spoke about what they wanted most from the Wizard of Oz. Dorothy spoke about Kansas and how much she missed home.

Soon, the path took them to a forest.

As they walked through the forest, Dorothy saw a tiny wooden cottage ahead.

As she knocked on the door and saw the dirty windows, she knew that no one had been there in a long time.

'Gver'ere!'

A strange sound came from behind the cottage.

'What was that noise?' asked Scarecrow.

'Gver'ere!'

It sounded like a **muffled** voice.

Toto ran behind the cottage and barked at a tall man made completely out of **tin**. He was holding an axe above his head that had bits of **rust** all over it.

muffled - A sound that is quiet because something is covering where the sound is coming from.

tin - A silvery-white metal.

rust - An orange, reddish covering that forms over old metal.

'Oh no! Are you alright?' asked Dorothy, as she ran to the Tin Man's side.

'Goil gan,' said the Tin Man. Dorothy didn't understand.

'I think he means, **oil can**,' said Scarecrow.

Hidden in the leaves, there was an **oil can**. Dorothy began **oiling** the Tin Man's body.

oil can - *A metal jug used to carry oil. (Oil is a black, shiny liquid sometimes used to help rusty metal move.)*

oiling - *To put oil on a rusty or stiff metal. Oil helps the metal to move and bend at its joints.*

Tin Man began to squeak and creak as he started to move. Eventually, he could move his lips.

'Thank you,' he said. 'I was chopping wood a year ago when it started to rain. The rain made me rust, and I have been stuck here ever since.'

Tin Man began to stretch. Soon, he was able to walk again.

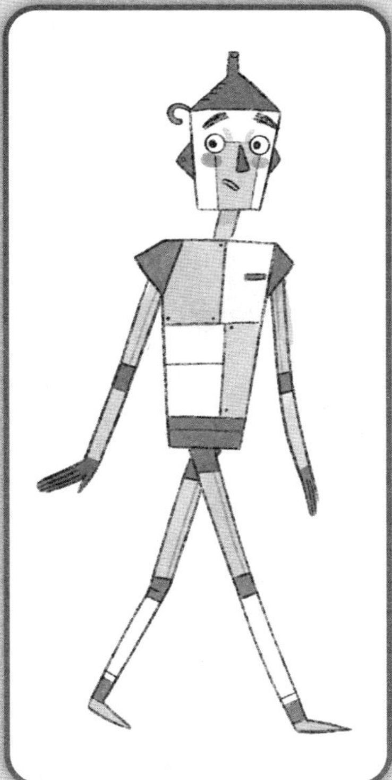

Then, Dorothy and Scarecrow told Tin Man what had happened and where they were going.

'The Wizard of Oz is going to help you get home, Dorothy?' asked Tin Man.

'And give me a brain!' said Scarecrow.

'Perhaps the Wizard will give me a heart,' said Tin Man.

'You don't have a heart?' asked Dorothy.

'I wish I did,' said Tin Man.

Dorothy and Scarecrow invited Tin Man to join them.

With Toto walking beside them, Dorothy and her two new friends carried on walking along the Yellow Brick Road.

The day turned to night. Dorothy carried Toto in her arms. The Yellow Brick Road was still leading them through the forest. It became scary and filled with shadows.

'What animals live in the forest?' asked Dorothy nervously.

'There are lions, tigers and maybe even bears,' warned Tin Man.

'Lions?' she repeated.
'And tigers? And bears?'

Just then, a loud roar came from deep inside the forest.

Chapter 4

Dorothy was scared. They heard another loud roar. Toto jumped out of Dorothy's arms and ran towards the noise.

'Toto! Come back!' shouted Dorothy.

Another frightening roar filled the forest.

Toto came running out of the trees chased by a huge Lion. The Lion roared at the little dog as Toto jumped into Dorothy's arms.

The Lion ran closer towards them. Dorothy reached out and hit it on its nose. She thought the lion would roar and **bare its sharp white teeth**.

Instead, it moaned, 'Ouch! What did you do that for?'

bare its sharp white teeth - To show sharp teeth to scare someone during or before a fight.

'You scared my dog!' Dorothy shouted angrily. 'You're a great big lion and Toto is only small.'

Lion began to cry. Huge tears dripped down his furry face.

'I'm sorry!' he **sobbed**. 'I'm just a big **coward**. I'm scared of everything in this forest that is bigger than your little dog.'

sobbed - When someone cries very loudly.

coward - When someone is afraid and scared of lots of things.

Dorothy felt **guilty**. She put her arm around Lion's shoulder.

'I am sorry for hitting your nose,' she said.

As Lion began to stop crying, he said, 'I wish I was brave.'

'Why don't you come with us to meet the Wizard of Oz?' suggested Tin Man. 'I'm sure the Wizard could help you find **courage**.'

guilty - When someone feels bad about something they have done.

courage - To be able to do something that is scary or frightening.

'If I had courage, I could be the king of the forest!' he said as he **paced**.

'As long as you don't frighten any more **creatures**,' said Dorothy. 'Sometimes being brave means being kind.'

Lion nodded and bowed his head. He had learnt his lesson.

'Let's get going!' Lion said.

paced - Walking at a steady speed, back and forth.

creatures - A living thing, like an animal.

The next morning, they finally reached the end of the forest.

Dorothy was amazed at the beautiful view ahead!

The Emerald City sparkled a beautiful green. It was **surrounded** by fields filled with pretty red flowers.

surrounded - When something is all around.

'We're nearly there!' said Dorothy in excitement. 'We just have to follow the Yellow Brick Road through this field of poppies!'

'Wait!' shouted Scarecrow.

'These are Oz poppies! They will make you fall asleep if you breathe too close to them.'

Dorothy began to feel sleepy. Toto was already asleep. She picked him up and hurried out of the field.

'It's a good job we're made out of tin and straw,' said Tin Man.

'But what about him?' asked Scarecrow.

They all turned and looked back to the field. There was Lion, fast asleep, snoring loudly.

They couldn't just leave Lion asleep in the poppy field! How could they help him?

'I have an idea!' said Tin Man. He then put his tin fingers in his mouth and made a whistling sound. It was the loudest noise Dorothy had ever heard!

After a few minutes, a tiny white mouse wearing a crown appeared.

The tiny mouse ran up Tin Man's arm and sat on his shoulder.

'Thank you for coming, Your **Majesty**,' said Tin Man. 'Please could you help my friend over there?' He pointed to sleeping Lion. The mouse nodded and ran away.

Tin Man smiled and explained that he had once helped the Queen of the Mice. She had said that one day, she would help him too.

Majesty - The word you call someone with power like a king or a queen.

Dorothy wondered how a mouse was going to move a lion!

Suddenly, they heard a loud **scurrying** noise. Hundreds of mice ran into the poppy field. They gently lifted Lion and carried him across the field, laying him next to Tin Man.

Tin Man thanked the Queen of the Mice. Then she and the mice ran back to the forest.

scurrying - To move quickly with small steps.

Chapter 5

Once Lion had woken from his sleep, the friends tried to decide how they were going to get to the Emerald City.

The Yellow Brick Road ran straight through the poppy field. They had no choice but to walk through it. But they had to think of a way of not breathing too close to the poppies, otherwise they would fall asleep.

'What if you rode on Lion's back?' said Scarecrow. 'Lion would have to run very fast and you would all need to hold your breath!'

'Great idea!' agreed Lion.

Dorothy climbed on Lion's back. She tucked Toto under her arm and held tightly onto Lion's mane.

They took a deep breath as Lion ran through the field.

Lion ran very fast! Soon, they were on the other side of the field, breathing in fresh air.

Scarecrow and Tin Man joined them as Dorothy looked up at the huge gates of the Emerald City.

She pushed the gates, but they didn't open. Even when all four of the friends pushed the gates, they stayed shut.

'Who's there?' shouted a man from the other side of the gates.

'I'm Dorothy. My friends and I have come to meet the Wizard of Oz,' said Dorothy.

She heard the man laugh.

'No one sees the Wizard! He is far too magical to meet you!' said the man.

'But Dorothy is magical!' said the Scarecrow. 'She killed the Wicked Witch of the East and has the witch's magical shoes. Look!'

He pointed to Dorothy's sparkling, silver shoes.

'Why didn't you say that before? Come on in!' the **gatekeeper** said. 'I'll send a message to the Wizard.'

He opened the gates.

gatekeeper - A person who controls who goes through a gate.

Dorothy and her friends stepped into the Emerald City. They had never seen anything like it.

Everything was green. The houses, paths and roads were all shining green. Everything was decorated with **emeralds**. Even the sky was green.

The people inside the city were friendly and excited to welcome them.

emeralds - A bright green gem stone.

The people of the Emerald City told the four friends all about the Wizard. He came to the city many years ago and made it into a happy and magical place.

Everyone loved the Wizard but no one seemed to know what he looked like! Some said he had the face of a tiger with purple eyes! Others said he was tall with long hair!

Dorothy, Tin Man, Scarecrow and Lion stood nervously in front of the door leading to the Wizard's room.

The gatekeeper appeared, pointed to Dorothy and shouted, 'Come on! You first!' He led her inside.

The Wizard's room was huge.
It had a shiny green floor, green curtains that hung from the ceiling to the floor and chairs with emerald decorations.

As Dorothy looked around,
a huge **floating** head appeared
in front of her!

'I am the great and powerful Wizard of Oz!' **boomed** the head.

'What do you want from me?' asked the head. 'And where did you get those sparkling shoes?'

floating - To fly slowly in the air.

boomed - A loud, low sound.

Dorothy looked down at the sparkling silver shoes.

'I got these shoes from the Wicked Witch of the East. My house fell on her and killed her,' she explained. 'I wish for you to send me back home to Kansas. My Aunt and Uncle will be very worried.'

The floating head stared at Dorothy, thinking about what it would do.

'I will **grant** your wish,' said the head. 'But only if you kill the Wicked Witch of the West, just like you killed her sister!'

'But I didn't kill her!' cried Dorothy. 'It was my house!'

'Do this!' shouted the head. 'And bring me her magical golden hat to prove it.'

The floating head then disappeared.

grant - To give.

Dorothy felt sad. How could she kill anyone?

She watched as the Scarecrow, Tin Man and Lion were taken into the Wizard's room. Everyone was told the same thing.

The Wizard would grant their wishes, only if they killed the Wicked Witch of the West.

Chapter 6

'I can't kill anyone!' Dorothy cried. 'I'm only a little girl!'

'I know,' said Scarecrow, giving Dorothy a hug. 'But we must all do as the fairy asked.'

'Fairy?' asked Dorothy. Scarecrow explained that the Wizard looked like a beautiful fairy.

Dorothy was confused.

Tin Man was confused too! He said the Wizard looked like a furry monster.

Lion said, 'You're all wrong! The Wizard was a ball of fire!'

It seemed that the Wizard changed what they looked like every time they met somebody new!

Dorothy just wanted to go home.

The gatekeeper appeared again.

'Come on!' he said. 'The Witch's castle is to the west of the Emerald City.'

The friends had no choice. If they wanted their wishes to be granted, they had to do what the Wizard said.

Dorothy, Scarecrow, Tin Man and Lion began their **journey** to the Witch's castle.

The road was very different to the Yellow Brick Road. It was dark. The trees had no leaves, and black birds flew over their heads.

Thick dark fog surrounded them, making it hard to see what was in front of them.

journey - *When someone travels from one place to another.*

'Look,' whispered Lion, as the fog disappeared. 'Up ahead ...'

The friends all stopped and looked at the tall, dark castle on a hill in front of them. Its twisting towers rose into the clouds.

'The Wicked Witch of the West's castle,' said Dorothy nervously.

Inside the castle, the Wicked Witch of the West was stood in front of her magical, golden hat.

She whispered a spell and the hat suddenly filled with pictures. The pictures showed Dorothy, Toto, Scarecrow, Tin Man and Lion.

The Wicked Witch of the West could see the friends walking along the path that led to the castle.

The Wicked Witch of the West looked closely at the pictures. She saw that Dorothy was wearing her sister's sparkling shoes!

'She has come to my castle wearing my sister's shoes!' the witch shouted angrily.

'I'm going to get my **revenge** on that little girl!' she **cackled**.

revenge - *When someone wants to hurt someone else because that person hurt them.*

cackled - *An evil and loud laugh.*

The Witch put her hands in the air and said, 'Come to me my friends!'

All at once, the room was filled with flying monkeys. They flew around the room. The witch had an evil smile.

'Find the girl with the silver shoes, and bring her to me!' she **commanded**.

commanded - *To give a firm instruction or order.*

'Get rid of the scarecrow and the man made with tin,' the Witch ordered. '*But*, bring the lion! I have always wanted a lion for my castle.'

The Witch smiled a wicked smile.

'Now fly!' she shouted.

The Witch lifted her hands and the windows of her tower opened. The monkeys flew into the foggy skies.

The four friends had been walking for a long time. They were feeling tired.

Dorothy looked towards the castle ahead. It looked like a dark cloud was flying towards them.

'Flying monkeys!' shouted Scarecrow.

The cloud was made of flying monkeys heading straight towards them!

Chapter 7

Lion stood on his back legs.

He roared and hit at the monkeys with his giant paws.

The monkeys grabbed and pinched at the friends as they tried to escape.

But it didn't work.

The monkeys took Scarecrow and Tin Man away.

'No!' cried Dorothy.

Toto barked as a large monkey lifted Dorothy up and flew with her into the sky.

Dorothy screamed as the monkeys grabbed Toto and Lion too.

Dorothy was **terrified** as they flew higher into the sky, her silver shoes sparkling beneath her.

terrified - *Very scared.*

The monkeys flew through the windows of the tower with Dorothy, Lion and Toto.

'Well done!' the witch cackled. 'Now leave!' The monkeys disappeared through the window.

The witch walked towards Dorothy.

'Hmm, what to do with you?' she asked.

Lion stepped between Dorothy and the Wicked Witch. He **snarled**.

'There's no need to **snarl** at your new owner!' laughed the witch.

The witch grabbed her golden hat and waved her hands, casting a spell.

There was a flash of light so bright that Dorothy covered her eyes.

snarled / snarl - An angry and scary growl.

When she opened her eyes, Lion was trapped inside a cage. He was roaring in anger.

'No!' cried Dorothy.

'Why shouldn't I lock up your friends when you killed my sister?' shouted the witch angrily.

'I didn't mean to do it!' said Dorothy.

'But now you are here to kill me!' said the witch.

Dorothy explained that the Wizard wanted the witch dead, but the only thing Dorothy wanted was the witch's golden hat.

'Give you my golden hat?' she said. 'Never! It's time for you to give me my sister's shoes.'

The Wicked Witch knew that the person wearing the silver shoes was protected by them.

This meant that the Wicked Witch couldn't use her magic on Dorothy.

The only way to get the shoes would be for Dorothy to hand them over or to take them off her feet.

Dorothy picked up Toto and held him close. She remembered what the Good Witch had said. She should never give her silver shoes to the Wicked Witch.

Dorothy looked around the tower for anything that could help her.
The only thing she could see was a dirty bucket of water and a mop.

Suddenly, the Wicked Witch **lunged** at Dorothy's feet. Without thinking, Dorothy grabbed the bucket and threw the dirty water over the witch.

Something strange began to happen. **Steam** came out of the witch's long dark hair and clothes.

'I'm melting!' she cried.

Dorothy watched as the witch disappeared, melting into nothing.

lunged - To move forward very quickly.

Steam - When water becomes very hot and turns into tiny drops in the air that look like clouds.

Once the Wicked Witch had disappeared, so did Lion's cage. Lion ran towards Dorothy, rubbing his huge mane against her.

'You killed the Wicked Witch of the West!' said Lion.

Dorothy looked at the empty clothes.

'I did,' she said. Just then, the flying monkeys flew back into the room. Lion roared at them in anger.

Dorothy looked at the monkeys.

Wait,' she said quietly. 'Look...'

The monkeys were all bowing to her.

'Thank you!' said the largest monkey.
'You have killed the Wicked Witch
of the West. She kept us prisoner
and made us work for her.
You have freed us!'

Dorothy smiled at them.

'How can we help you?' said the large monkey.

Dorothy explained that she wanted to be back with her friends and get to the Emerald City. The monkeys agreed to take them all back to see the Wizard.

Just before they left, Lion picked up the witch's golden hat and gave it to Dorothy. Now they could give it to the Wizard of Oz.

Chapter 8

The monkeys kept their promise. They found Scarecrow and Tin Man and flew them all back to the Emerald City.

As they landed, they waved goodbye to the monkeys who were finally free from the Wicked Witch of the West.

'We did it!' cheered Dorothy, holding the golden hat and smiling at her friends.

The four friends went to the wizard's room. They were excited to finally get their wishes.

The gatekeeper wasn't there. They were unsure what to do so they knocked on the wizard's door.

As Lion knocked on the door, it opened. The four friends slowly walked into the room.

'Hello?' Dorothy called into the dark room.

'Who's there?' said a shocked voice.

'It's Dorothy. We've come to see the Wizard,' she answered.

All of a sudden, the room filled with light. Images started to appear, one after the other. At first a head, then a fairy, then a monster and finally a ball of fire.

'Go away! The Wizard will not see you!' the voice shouted.

'But why? The Wicked Witch of the West is gone. We have her golden hat!' cried Dorothy.

She put Toto on the floor.
She was so angry!

Toto ran to the curtains and pulled them with his mouth. As he pulled the curtains, they fell to the floor.

Behind the curtains, was an old man standing in front of a microphone and lights.

'Who are you?' asked Scarecrow.

'I am Oz, the Great and Powerful,' sighed the old man.

'You are the Wizard?' asked Dorothy. She couldn't believe it. The old, short man didn't look like a wizard at all.

'Yes,' replied the Wizard. 'Many years ago, I worked for a Circus in **Nebraska**.

I was in charge of the **hot air balloon** rides. One day, my balloon got caught in a strong wind and it landed here in the land of Oz.

The people in Oz thought I was a wizard because I could do a few circus tricks.'

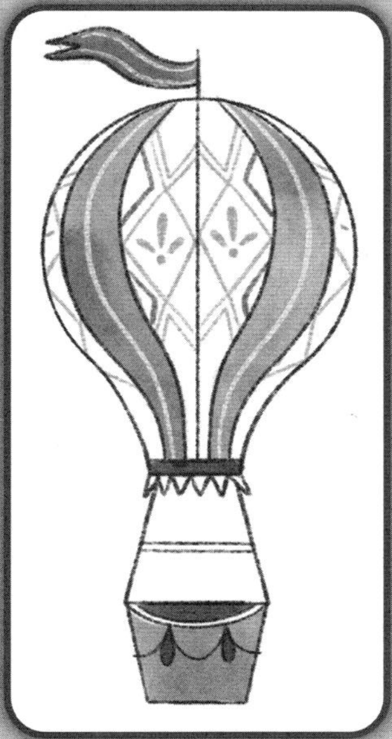

Nebraska - A state in the middle of the USA.

hot air balloon - A huge balloon with a basket underneath that people can travel in.

'Soon, I became the **leader** of the Emerald City. I think I have done a good job.

But now I am getting older. I worry that the people will realise that I'm not a real wizard.

I **feared** that once the witches found out, they would come for me and take over Oz,' said the wizard.

leader - The person who makes the rules and makes sure people follow them.

feared - To be scared of something.

'So, you are a liar?' asked Tin Man. 'You can't give us our wishes?'

Dorothy felt so sad. The only thing she wanted was to go home.

'I'm sorry,' said the Wizard. 'I used my lamps and **puppets** to make all the images you saw. They helped me to look like a magical wizard.'

puppets - A toy of a person or animal which can be moved by a hand inside it or by strings.

'Can't you help any of us?' asked Dorothy.

The Wizard remembered Scarecrow wanted a brain. So, he gave Scarecrow a rolled-up piece of paper tied with a ribbon.

'Without a brain, you could not have helped Dorothy,' said the Wizard. 'Here is a **qualification** to show everyone that you have a brain!'

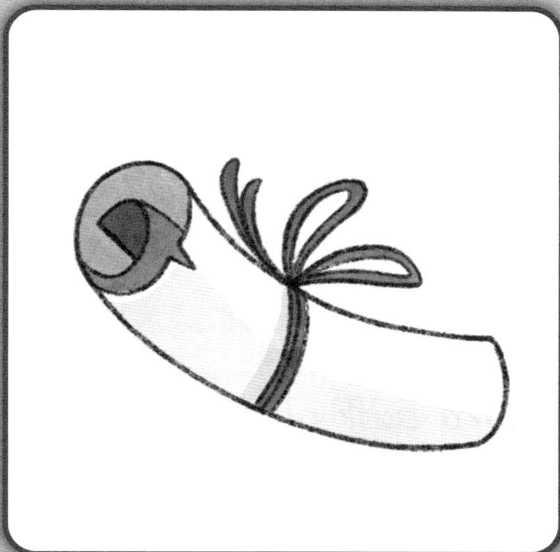

qualification - *Paper with important facts saying someone has passed a test or exam.*

Next, the Wizard turned to Tin Man.

'You have been a good friend to Dorothy,' said the Wizard. 'But you cannot be a friend without a heart.'

The Wizard took out a red **handkerchief** from his pocket and folded it into a heart shape.

He gave it to Tin Man who smiled and held it close to his tin chest.

handkerchief - A small cloth used for wiping a person's nose.

'As for you, Lion,' said the Wizard. 'You must have courage because you helped to kill the witch.'

'I think you need a medal for being so brave!' said the Wizard, handing Lion a **pocket watch**.

Lion hung the **pocket watch** around his neck **proudly**.

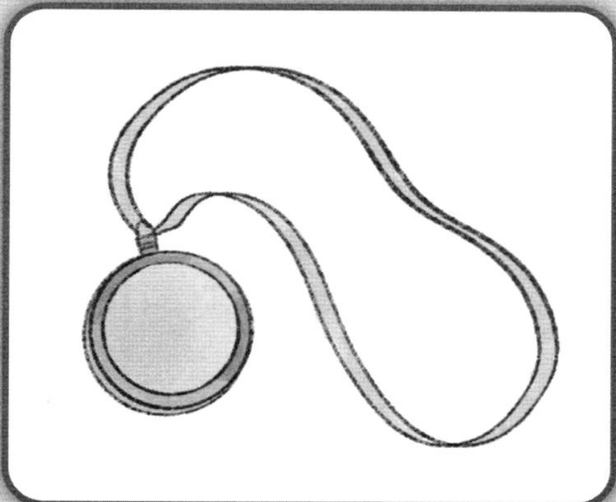

pocket watch - A watch on a chain that is usually carried in a pocket.

proudly - The way someone does something when they are happy with their choices.

'What about Dorothy?' asked Scarecrow.

Dorothy looked sadly at Toto. How was the Wizard going to help her?

He walked past them and pulled down more of the curtains. Behind them was a large basket, attached to a huge piece of colourful material.

'This is my hot air balloon. It can take you home,' said the Wizard.

'I can't fly a hot air balloon!' said Dorothy.

'That's why I am coming with you,' said the Wizard. 'It is time I left the people of Oz.'

The Wizard of Oz began to drag the hot air balloon and its basket out of the room.

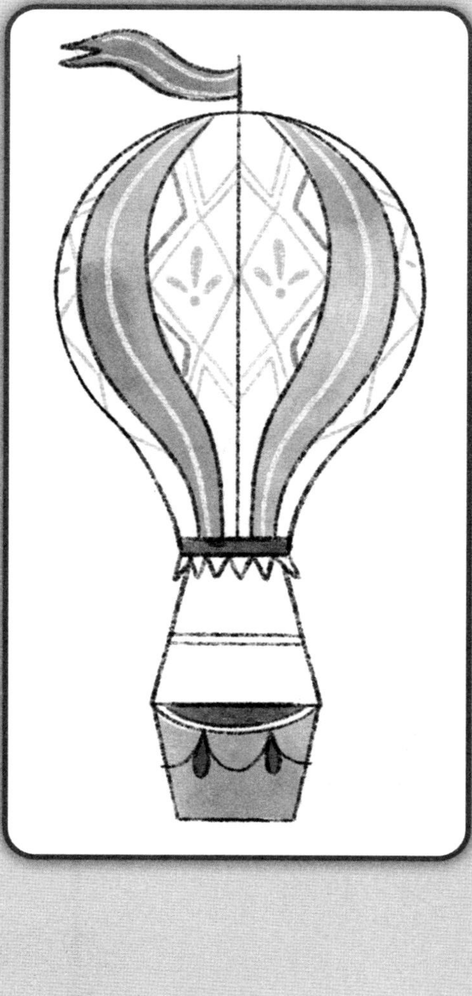

Scarecrow, Tin Man and Lion followed the Wizard.

'But who will be in charge of Oz if you leave?' asked Scarecrow.

'I think you three will be the best to lead,' he said. 'Scarecrow has a brain, Tin Man has a heart and Lion has courage. Together you will keep the Emerald City safe.'

The four friends helped the Wizard to lift the hot air balloon out into the **town square** of the Emerald City.

A crowd had gathered to watch.

The Wizard told the people that it was time he went home, but he was leaving them with three new leaders. He pointed to Scarecrow, Tin Man and Lion. Everyone cheered.

town square - *An open space in the centre of a town.*

Chapter 9

As the Wizard of Oz got into the hot air balloon, Dorothy knew it was time to say goodbye.

'Goodbye, Lion. Thank you for being so brave,' she said, giving Lion a hug.

Next, she stretched up to kiss Tin Man's cheek and said, 'I have never met anyone with such a kind heart.'

She then turned to Scarecrow, hugged him and whispered, 'I think I will miss you most of all.'

'Come on, Dorothy! We are about to leave!' called the Wizard.

Dorothy was just about to climb into the balloon's basket, but she couldn't find Toto.

'I can't leave without Toto!' she cried.

The hot air balloon had begun to rise into the sky.

'Dorothy! Quickly!' shouted the Wizard, as the balloon rose even higher.

Dorothy and her friends searched for Toto. When Dorothy finally found Toto, it was too late. The balloon had gone. Her only way home had left the Emerald City without her.

'Now what will I do?' she sobbed.

'You can stay here with us,' said Scarecrow.

'I love you all,' she said with a sad smile. 'But there is no place like home.'

At that moment, a bright sparkling light appeared in the town square.

Suddenly, another witch appeared!

It was Glinda, the Good Witch of the South. The people felt excited because Glinda was kind.

She floated towards Dorothy, carrying a wand that shone with golden sparkles.

'Why do you look so sad, child?' she asked.

Dorothy turned to the witch. 'I want to go home. I'm afraid I will be stuck here forever,' she cried.

The witch smiled and said,
'But you've had the power to get home all along.'

Dorothy looked confused.

'Tap your heels together three times, wish really hard and say what you want most,' said the witch.

Dorothy smiled. She looked at her new friends. They had all found what they wanted. But they had those things all along, they just didn't know it. She could leave them knowing they were happy.

She picked up Toto and closed her eyes.

She tapped her heels together three times and said, 'Take me home!'

Dorothy opened her eyes.

Uncle Henry and Aunt Em's house was right in front of her.

The door was broken and the roof was missing some tiles, but it was now back home in Kansas. Dorothy and Toto were no longer in the Land of Oz.

'Dorothy!' cried Aunt Em. She looked so happy.

Dorothy ran towards her and hugged her.

'Where have you been?' asked Aunt Em.

'I have been far away,' said Dorothy. 'But I am so glad to be home!'

That very same day, somewhere in a **desert** far away, two shoes landed in the sand.

They **glittered** in the sun and were lost forever.

desert - *A very hot place with sand everywhere.*

glittered - *To shine brightly.*

L. Frank Baum

In 1856, Frank Baum was born in New York. When Baum was young, he was often very ill. But he still loved acting and writing.

In 1900, he wrote *The Wonderful Wizard of Oz*. Since then, it has been made into many plays, films and musicals.